Published by Scholastic Inc.
90 Old Sherman Turnpike, Danbury, Connecticut 06816.

For information regarding permission, write to:
Disney Licensed Publishing
114 Fifth Avenue, New York, New York 10011.

ISBN 0-7172-6815-2

Designed and produced by Bill SMITH STUDIO.

Printed in the U.S.A.
First printing, March 2004

A Green Thumb

A Story About
Being Humble

by **Jacqueline A. Ball**
illustrated by
Teresa Lester *with*
S.I. International

SCHOLASTIC INC.

New York   Toronto   London   Auckland   Sydney
Mexico City   New Delhi   Hong Kong   Buenos Aires

"*A*unt Fauna! Aunt Merryweather!" exclaimed Briar Rose. "Aunt Flora has finished her basket! Come and see!"

"It's beautiful!" said Merryweather.

"You must be so proud, Flora," said Fauna.

"With a little time and patience, anyone could have done it," Flora replied. "And all these rainy days have given me plenty of time!"

"You're being too humble," Fauna said. "You're a wonderful basket-weaver."

*B*riar Rose reached for a warm roll and took a bite. "Delicious," she said. "Nobody bakes like you, Aunt Merryweather."

"That's kind of you, dear," Merryweather answered. "But it's easy once you know how."

The sun peeked through the windows.

"The sun is out," said Briar Rose. "Finally! Let's go check our gardens. I'm sure we'll have plenty of weeds to pull after so many rainy days."

In the spring, each of her aunts had planted a vegetable patch. Briar Rose had planted flowers.

"My radishes should be nice and plump by now," said Flora.

"I can't wait to see my eggplants," said Merryweather. She and Flora hurried to the door.

Fauna sat quietly.

"What's wrong?" Briar Rose asked her.

$\mathcal{F}$auna smiled and shrugged. "I don't have much luck with vegetables. Last year, Merryweather's carrots were twice the size of mine. The year before, wiggleworms ate holes in my cabbages but didn't touch Flora's."

"Maybe this summer things will be different," comforted Briar Rose.

"Maybe," said Fauna. "But I doubt it."

They walked to the garden. Fauna suddenly gasped and grabbed Briar Rose's hand. "Look!"

FAUNA

BRIAR ROSE

MERRYWEATHER

FLORA

Briar Rose followed her gaze to a row of bean plants. Merryweather and Flora were gazing in the same direction.

FAUNA

BRIAR ROSE

MERRYWEATHER

FLORA

"My bean plants!" Fauna exclaimed. "They're so . . ."

"Tall," finished Merryweather, brushing a swarm of bugs off an eggplant covered with holes.

FAUNA

BRIAR ROSE

MERRYWEATHER

FLORA

$\mathcal{F}$auna touched one of the plants in wonder. "It looks so . . . "

"Healthy," finished Flora. Then she looked at the soggy, limp radishes in her hand.

"Just wait," Briar Rose encouraged Flora and Merryweather. "Your plants are sure to improve, now that the sun has come out." The sun shone brightly all afternoon.

FAUNA

BRIAR ROSE

The next morning, everyone trooped out to the garden. This time, Fauna eagerly led the way.

Flora's radishes were scrawnier. Armies of bugs marched over Merryweather's eggplants. But Fauna's plants looked even healthier. And they were loaded with beans.

FLORA

$\mathcal{A}$ huge smile lit up Fauna's face. She picked a bean and nibbled. "It's crisp and crunchy!"

She picked more beans and gave them to the others. "Here, taste. Aren't they good?"

"They're perfect," Briar Rose agreed after eating one. "Good for you, Aunt Fauna!"

"Yes, congratulations," murmured Flora, her disappointed gaze returning to her radishes.

"Yes, how nice for you," agreed Merryweather. She looked sadly at her eggplants.

The plant labels visible in the illustration read: FAUNA, MERRYWEATHER, BRIAR ROSE, FLORA

*F*auna's bean plants grew and grew. Day after day, she watered them and carefully polished their leaves.

The others took care of their plants, too.
But still, theirs did not grow like Fauna's.

$\mathcal{B}$riar Rose was glad for Fauna's success. "You seem to have a green thumb after all," she told Fauna.

"I guess so," said Fauna, shaking her head in disbelief.

But Briar Rose was becoming worried about
Flora and Merryweather. Instead of being happy
for Fauna's success, they seemed upset.

Fauna raced to the garden every day at sunrise and stayed for hours, tending her beans.

Meanwhile, Merryweather and Flora had almost given up on their gardens.

*F*auna felt sad that their plants hadn't done as well as hers. "Maybe I can help," she thought. So she began to offer gentle advice.

"Perhaps if you weeded more, your radishes would grow better, Flora. And if you didn't water your eggplants so much, Merryweather, the bugs might stay away."

Eventually, Fauna's bushes produced
hundreds of beans. Fauna carried basket after basket
into the house. "I've never seen so many beans," she
said gaily. "Those bushes just won't stop!"

She didn't notice Merryweather's frown.

$\mathcal{F}$auna's beans became part of every meal.

"It's a good thing we all like them," Fauna said cheerfully.

She didn't hear Flora's loud sigh.

$\mathcal{T}$hen one summer day, Fauna decided to paint a picture of some of her beans. "So even in the winter, we can remember how they looked," she explained, carrying her easel and paints outside.

Meanwhile, inside the cottage, Flora was busy weaving a new basket. "I'm so tired of hearing about those beans," she muttered.

"I am, too," Merryweather said, taking a batch of rolls from the oven. "Fauna never stops bragging about them."

Briar Rose entered the room in time to hear them.

What would a princess do?

She put her arms around her aunts and spoke kindly. "You know, Aunt Fauna is always thrilled at your successes at basket-weaving and baking. But now she's happy to have some success of her own."

"*I* hadn't thought about it that way," Flora said quietly.

"Of course Fauna deserves her own success," agreed Merryweather.

*B*riar Rose took a roll out to Fauna.

"Thank you, Briar Rose," Fauna said. "My, that smells delicious!"

Eagerly Fauna showed Briar Rose her painting. "I think I'll hang it over the fireplace so we can always see it."

"The picture is lovely, Aunt Fauna, and I'm so happy for your success," Briar Rose said in a soft, gentle voice. "But do you think being reminded of your good fortune might make others feel bad?"

"*I* suppose it could," Fauna replied slowly, looking at her painting.

Then her face brightened. "Thanks, Briar Rose, you've given me an idea."

$\mathcal{A}$ few days later, Fauna called the others together. "I'm sorry if I seemed to be bragging," she said. "But now I've painted a new picture."

Fauna's painting now showed Flora's basket, Merryweather's rolls, Briar Rose's flowers, as well as one of Fauna's bean bushes.

"*I*t's wonderful!" exclaimed Briar Rose.

"We're truly glad your beans were such a success, Fauna," Merryweather and Flora said.

"Now we have something to remind us all of this special summer," said Briar Rose with a smile.

The End